EMILY CARR'S WOO

Emily Carr's Woo

by
Constance Horne

Illustrated by
Lissa Calvert

oolichan books
LANTZVILLE, BRITISH COLUMBIA, CANADA
1995

The cover portrait "Woo" by Emily Carr is used by permission of the B.C. Archives and Records Service.

Canadian Cataloguing in Publication Data

Horne, Constance.
Emily Carr's Woo
ISBN 0-88982-149-6

1. Carr, Emily, 1871-1945—Juvenile fiction. 2. Woo (Monkey)—Juvenile fiction. I. Title.
PS8565.O6693E44 1995   jC813'.54   C95-910767-3
PZ7.H67Em 1995

Publication of this book has been financially assisted by The Canada Council.

Published by
oolichan books
P.O. Box 10
Lantzville, B.C.
Canada V0R 2H0

Printed in Canada by
Best Books

To my husband
Ted Horne

Woo packs her tin box

Contents

CHAPTER ONE

Not Another Pet!

Emily Carr was nervous. Her sisters were coming to dinner. As she moved back and forth setting the table, she kept glancing into a dark corner of the studio. Many paintings were stored there. And so was something else. Oh, Alice and Lizzie were going to scold her!

She heard their voices as they began to climb the outside staircase. Each of the Carr sisters owned a house near the sea in Victoria, British Columbia. Emily's, called Hill House, was divided into apartments. She lived and painted in the one on the top floor, at the back. It was a long climb up from the garden.

The old ladies were panting slightly when they stepped into Emily's studio. For a moment they stood sniffing the roast beef smell and smiling at one another.

Alice took off her hat and hung it on a peg.

"Where are the dogs?" she asked.

"In the yard," Emily answered.

Alice raised her eyebrows in surprise. At least three griffons were usually present at her younger sister's parties.

Lizzie looked sharply at the table.

"Where's the rat?" she asked.

"Shut up in the attic," Emily said. "I know you don't like Suzie to be on the table at meals."

"Humph," said Lizzie. "That never stopped you before."

"Hello! Hello! Say hello to Jane," a voice squawked.

Alice laughed and walked over to the window where a green parrot paced to and fro on her perch.

"Hello, Jane," she said.

"Hello! Hello!" repeated Jane. "Bad girl! Bad girl!"

"Why, you cheeky thing!" said Alice.

"Don't be rude, Jane," called Emily. "She doesn't mean you, Alice. Come to the table. Dinner is ready."

For the next few minutes, the scraping of knives and forks and the chatter of the three sisters covered the sounds coming from the other side of the room. Then, while Emily poured tea, there was a pause. All three women heard a whimper. "Woo, woo."

Emily rattled her tea cup in the saucer to drown out the sound but Lizzie was not fooled.

"What's that?" she demanded.

Emily smiled weakly.

"I have a new pet," she said.

"Millie! Not another," said Alice with a sigh.

"What is it this time?" asked Lizzie in a hard voice.

Emily padded over to the corner of the studio, reached behind a stack of pictures and lifted out an old round birdcage with metal bars. She placed it on the floor well away from the table.

"Woo, woo," said the creature in the cage.

Lizzie twisted around in her chair. Her eyes widened. Her mouth dropped open.

Alice jumped up and took three steps forward. She pushed her glasses up on her forehead and then pulled them down again.

"It's a monkey!" she gasped.

"Yes," said Emily. "She's a Javanese monkey. Isn't she beautiful?"

The little creature squatted on the bottom of the cage. Her long black hands clung to two of the bars and her skinny tail was wrapped around another. The tail, like the rest of her thin body, was covered with greeny-brown fur. She had a small, pointed face with a tuft of light-coloured whiskers on each cheek. Bushy eyebrows over dark, staring eyes made her look quite fierce.

"Beautiful?" asked Lizzie in disgust. "It's horrid! Worse than the rat."

The monkey opened her jaws very wide and showed her strong white teeth. Emily, who was still standing beside the cage, could see right down her throat to where the yowl came from. She laughed.

"Careful, Lizzie," she said. "She understands English."

She went back to sit at the table.

"Where did it come from?" asked Lizzie.

"From the pet store."

"You bought it?" exclaimed Lizzie in amazement. "How can you afford a monkey?"

All this time, the parrot had been pacing back and forth along her perch. Now she shrieked, "Bad girl! Bad girl!"

Emily glared at the bird before answering her sister.

"It was a straight trade. The shop owner is going to take a griffon pup from the next litter."

Lizzie groaned and shook her head.

"You can't keep a monkey, Millie," said Alice in the tone she used to reason with the children in her school. "She'll wreck the house."

"She'll tease the dogs," warned Lizzie.

"She'll bother the tenants. They'll leave," said Alice.

"Bad girl! Bad girl!" squawked Jane.

The two old ladies talked on and on, thinking up more and more reasons why owning a monkey would be a mistake.

Emily just sat there, elbows firmly on the table, jaws clenched and eyes blazing. Her sisters knew that stubborn look. They gave up.

The parrot tried one more time.

"Bad girl!" she said.

Suddenly, the monkey stood up to her full height. Her head touched the top of the cage. She stuck a leg out on one side and an arm on the other and scuttled across to the parrot's pole.

Alice and Emily burst out laughing.

Even Lizzie smiled. It was funny to see the cage moving around the room as the monkey explored the studio.

Later, the sisters prepared to leave.

"You'll see," said Alice. "She'll be too much trouble."

They went down the stairs.

"Send her back," called Lizzie from the bottom step. "You have enough animals."

Emily slammed the door shut. At the sharp sound, the monkey cowered against the bars of the cage. Emily lifted off the cover and cuddled the animal in her arms.

"Don't worry little monk. I don't have to listen to my big sisters anymore. I'm fifty-two years old. I own a house and a business. I'm an artist and some people think I'm a good one. Who cares what Alice and Lizzie say? You're mine and I'm going to keep you."

The monkey wrapped a long arm around Emily's neck and nestled her head under the woman's chin.

"Woo, woo," she whimpered.

Emily rubbed her cheek against the soft fur.

"Poor little mite. You're missing your monkey family."

"Woo, woo."

"That's what I'll call you," Emily said. "Woo, my dear little monkey."

CHAPTER TWO

Monkey Mischief

As time passed, Woo settled into her new home. She had her own corner of the basement with a cozy sleeping box and a windowsill where she could sit and watch what was happening on the front street. For warm nights, she had another sleeping box out in the back yard. From there, she could see the dogs in their run at the bottom of the garden.

Woo was wearing a leather collar when she came home from the pet shop. On the second day, Emily began to train the monkey to accept a chain attached to the collar. Even though she ignored her sisters' advice about keeping her new pet, Emily knew they were right about the trouble a loose monkey could cause. When Woo was indoors, the chain was short. In the garden, it was long so she could run and play. When Emily walked the dogs, Woo went along, too, chained to her owner's waist. Soon she became a member of Emily's animal family.

When winter came, Emily noticed that the monkey shivered a lot. And why not? She had come from a tropical island where the weather was always warm. It probably rained even more on Java than it did on Vancouver Island, but the rain there only made the jungle steamier. Even the winds were warm, unlike the cold breezes that came off the northern Pacific Ocean. Woo needed clothes.

Emily found a piece of flannelette, borrowed a doll's dress pattern, and made a pretty blue dress. It had puff sleeves, gathers at the waist, and a row of buttons down the front. After she had buttoned Woo into it, Emily smiled.

"Oh, you look pretty, Ma'am. Doesn't Woo look pretty, Jane?"

"Wrack! Wrack! Wrack!" said the parrot, nastily.

"Don't mind her, Woo," said Emily, as she left the room.

Woo took a step toward Jane's perch. The skirt of the dress tripped her.

"Wrack!" laughed Jane.

Woo tore at the skirt until it pulled away from the top. She chewed off the buttons and ripped out the sleeves. When her mistress returned in five minutes, Woo was wearing nothing but a blue flannelette ring around her neck.

The next dress was made of heavy woolen material. That one lasted half an hour. Finally, Emily made a wide dress of tough canvas and put the buttons in the back. The monkey couldn't rip that one or the others that Emily later made for her. Often she was allowed to choose which dress to wear on visits to Emily's sisters.

Woo wasn't welcome everywhere. One day, the three Carr sisters were invited to tea at the home of an old friend. Her house was full of beautiful furniture and china ornaments. No monkeys allowed there! Woo would have to stay home.

She and Jane and Emily were all in the kitchen when Alice Carr came panting in, carrying a basket of ripe tomatoes.

"Thanks," said Emily. "Put them on the table beside the salt and vinegar, will you?

I'll cook the chili sauce when I get home."

"The taxi will be here in ten minutes," warned Alice.

"I'm almost ready. I just have to fill the creatures' food dishes."

As Emily clipped a fresh cracker to Jane's perch, her sister gasped.

"Millie, you can't go like that!" she said. "Your hem's down."

"Is it? Drat! " said Emily. "I'll pin it up."

"You will not," declared Alice. "Go and sew it properly. I'll tend to the animals. Hurry! You know Lizzie hates to be kept waiting."

Woo jumped up on the counter where Alice was cutting an apple. She reached for a bright red tomato.

"No, Woo," said Alice firmly.

Next, Woo eyed the bobbing cherries on Alice's tea-party hat.

"No, Woo!" said Alice, even more firmly.

"Tie her up," called Emily from behind the bedroom door. "Her chain is on the table leg. Hook it to her collar."

Alice lured the monkey under the table with half an orange.

BEEP! BEEP!

"Oh, there's the taxi," said Alice.

She grabbed the end of Woo's chain and

fastened the clip. Neither she nor Woo knew that the clip did not catch properly.

As the two women hurried out, Emily called, "Be good, Woo. Be a good monkey."

The monkey gazed sulkily at the closed door for a few minutes. Then she shrugged and ate the orange. Her bright eyes darted all over the room looking for amusement.

She found it right above her head. The drawer in the table was not quite closed. Woo stood up to her full height and pulled it open. She reached in, took a spoon, and beat on the table top. She threw the spoon down. It made a lovely ringing sound. She grabbed another one and dropped it. Soon spoons, knives, and forks littered the floor.

"Bad girl! Bad girl!" squawked Jane from the far corner of the room.

Woo made a face at her.

"Braaaaack!" said Jane.

Woo had made friends with all the household pets except the parrot. They had been enemies since the first day. Knowing this, Emily always made sure that they were tethered far enough apart so that they could not reach each other even at the ends of their chains.

Both of them were smart enough to know this. So, Woo climbed up on the table and raced back and forth calling names at Jane. The parrot stalked back and forth along her perch and hurled insults at the monkey. Finally, Woo lost her temper completely and took a flying leap at the bird.

She landed at the base of the pole. Quickly, she scrambled up and clasped the perch. Fluttering her wings and scolding at the top of her voice, Jane pecked at the monkey's black hands.

Woo hung on with her feet and used her hands to bat at the parrot. She was careful to keep her head down to protect her eyes from that sharp beak. At last, she caught hold of a red and green tail feather. She yanked hard.

Jane screamed.

Woo dropped to the floor with the feather in her hand.

She jumped up and down, waving her trophy. She laughed and smirked and gloated.

Jane crouched on her perch, twisted her head to look at her tail, and whimpered. She began to preen her remaining tail feathers, all the time making mournful sounds.

Suddenly, Woo stopped laughing. She realized that she was free. Her chain lay on the floor amid all the cutlery. Chattering with excitement, she went exploring.

First to the tomatoes. She picked one up and took a dainty bite.

"Bad girl!" said Jane, in a subdued voice.

Woo flung the tomato at her.

It shattered against the wall in a starburst of red pulp and yellow seeds.

"Chee, chee, chee!" yelled Woo in delight.

She hurled another tomato. And another. And another, until all four walls were decorated and the basket was empty.

Then she attacked the paper sack beside the basket. Grains of coarse pickling salt dribbled out of the hole she made. She tasted them, spat them out quickly, and rubbed the back of her hand over her mouth.

"Bad girl!" said Jane, daringly.

Woo scooped up a handful of salt and threw it at her. None of it hit the bird, but in falling it made a pretty pattern on the floor.

Woo made the hole bigger and threw salt in a semicircle under the counter. She cocked her head from side to side and admired the effect. When Emily painted, she would stand back and study her canvas in just the same way.

By now, the sack was half empty. Woo tucked it under one arm and jumped to the floor. Holding the bag by one corner, she backed across the room dribbling a zigzag line of white until the salt was all gone. Then she returned to the counter to check the vinegar jar.

It was made of mottled brown stoneware and had a cork pushed firmly into the top. Woo's strong teeth soon pulled that out.

Phew! Bad smell! She pushed the bottle away. It tipped over, and a river of vinegar poured along the counter and onto the floor. Chattering happily, Woo tilted the jar until it, too, was empty.

Just then, Emily's voice called out from the bottom of the stairs.

"Hello, creatures! I'm home."

Jane danced in excitement.

Woo jumped down and scampered under the table. She picked up her chain from among the spoons and forks, shook off the salt and vinegar, and draped the end of it around her shoulders. Then she folded her hands in her lap and watched the closed door through which her mistress would come. As the voice came closer, she pursed up her lips for kissing.

Emily was still talking.

"You didn't miss a thing, little monk. It was a stupid party. Lots of silly people sitting around sipping . . . "

The door opened. Emily gasped.

"Oh! Oh! Woo! Bad monkey! Bad girl!"

Much, much later, when the kitchen was clean again, Emily sat on the couch in the studio with Woo in her lap. She stroked the soft body gently.

"I worked off all my mad," she said. "After all, you were only doing what comes naturally to monkeys. Anyway, I'm glad one of us had a happy day."

CHAPTER THREE

Friends

Woo was about two years old when she came to live at Hill House. At that time, Miss Carr was raising and selling griffon dogs. They were small animals, not much bigger than the monkey, with long grey or black hair and stubby tails. There were other pets, too: Jane the parrot, Suzie the white rat, and several cats.

The little monkey hated the parrot. She had nothing in common with the rat. The cats ignored her. The dogs had one another for company. Woo was lonely. She needed an animal companion as well as her human friend.

One warm day, shortly after she came,

Woo was sitting on the lower branch of the cherry tree watching the dogs play together. Three older dogs and one puppy chased one another round and round the garden, played leap-frog, and rolled in the grass. For a long time Woo sat perfectly still, watching them. When they next tumbled near her, she dropped down into the middle of the pack. The older dogs scampered out of reach of the monkey's chain, but Woo caught the pup, Ginger Pop, by the tail. She hung on till his frightened yips died away. Then she turned him around and forced him into a staring contest. The puppy blinked first. Woo made soft cooing noises at him. She gently combed his fur with her long fingers. Ginger Pop snuggled up to her. They were friends. From then on, the two youngsters grew up together, like children in a human family.

Ginger Pop was Woo's special friend, but she liked the other dogs, too. She also loved to tease them. One of her favourite tricks was to sneak up on a griffon and pull its tail. None of them could move fast enough to catch her. Sometimes, she would snatch a water dish from under a dog's nose, tilt it over her huge mouth, and pour down every drop. As the dog barked angrily, she'd squirt some of the water back in his face.

Emily would hear the commotion.

"Bad monk! Don't tease the dogs," she'd say.

To earn extra money, Miss Carr gave art lessons. One summer, she had a class of six children. Most of the children liked visiting the animals even more than they liked drawing and painting. They would come early and spend time petting the dogs, or talking to the parrot, or playing with the kittens, or stroking the rat. But the monkey was everybody's favourite.

One day, Allen and Betty arrived first. They were calling to Woo as they hurried into the back yard where the lessons took place. The monkey heard them and scampered up the cherry tree to which she was tethered.

"I see her," said Betty. "She's wearing her pink dress today."

Allen stood under the tree and held up a matchbox.

"I brought you a present, Woo," he said. "Come and see."

The monkey moved down to a lower branch and peered at the box. Allen opened it and put the contents between his two hands.

"Come and get a snack, Woo," coaxed Betty. "It's yummy. You'll like it. Mmmmm! Yummy!"

Woo moved closer.

The boy opened his hands and showed a shiny black beetle. When the monkey reached down to take it, he clapped his hands shut. Woo shrieked with rage.

Allen laughed and backed away.

"Come on, here it is," he said, showing the bug again.

Woo's lightning-fast lunge was stopped short by a pull on her collar. Betty had wrapped Woo's chain around her arm to prevent the monkey from getting her treat. She laughed mockingly.

"Poor Woo! Poor Woo!" she shouted.

Just then, Miss Carr appeared at the studio door.

"Don't tease the monkey," she called angrily. "If she gets mad, she'll bite you and your parents will make me punish her. It's not fair. Leave her alone."

Jeff, Dorothy, Prue, and Monica had arrived in time to see the end of this scene. While the other children helped Miss Carr set up the easels, Jeff rummaged in Woo's toy box. He found a lady's hand mirror and held it out to the whimpering animal.

"Here, Woo, play with this," he said gently.

After a long, hard stare, the monkey slowly lowered her arm. Then she snatched the mirror and swung up to a higher branch. Dororthy and Monica came to watch her talk to the monkey in the mirror. They laughed at her when she began to kiss the glass.

"Silly Woo!" yelled Dorothy. "It's only you!"

"Woo's dumb! Woo's dumb!" chanted Monica.

Jeff shoved her, but before Monica could hit him back, Miss Carr called them to their places. For about twenty minutes the children all worked quietly. They were drawing their teacher's square, grey pottery kiln and a row of orange bowls in front of it.

Prue couldn't get the curve of the second bowl right. After rubbing it out for the third time, she sat back and kicked her heels against the chair leg. A movement off to the left caught her eye.

The monkey was on the ground. Prue watched her turning over stones at the edge of the flower bed. Every once in a while, she'd pop a wood bug or an ant into her mouth. Prue heard the crunch of her jaws. She poked Allen with her pencil, pointed at Woo, and made a face of disgust. He grinned.

Prue checked on her teacher. Miss Carr had her back to them as she helped Monica. Prue broke off bits of her art eraser and shaped them so that they looked like insect eggs. She held them out to Allen and pointed to the stone just back of his chair.

He understood at once. That chair was as far as Woo's chain would reach. Otherwise she'd be a nuisance, squeezing paint tubes, upsetting water pots, or tearing paper. The boy stood up quietly and tip-toed to the stone. He placed the eraser bits under it and then eased back into his chair and pretended to go on drawing.

Woo, poised to run when the boy moved, kept her eye on him. When he had been quiet for a while, she went on with her search for food. Soon she came to Allen's rock. She flipped it over and gobbled down the creamy bits.

Pah! Pah! She spat them out.

The two children exploded in giggles. Miss Carr whipped around and saw the angry monkey racing back up the tree.

Her scolding was nearly as loud as Woo's.

At the end of the lesson, Miss Carr served lemonade and cookies. The children sat on the grass under Woo's tree while the monkey crouched above, glaring at them all from under her shaggy eyebrows. No matter how sweetly they called or how many cookies they offered, she wouldn't join them.

"Just ignore her, " said Miss Carr. "When she thinks we've forgotten her, she'll come to someone she likes."

"To me," boasted Prue. "She likes me best."

That started an argument. Who did Woo like best?

A branch creaked. They all looked up. Woo picked three cherries. She popped one into each of her cheek pouches. The third went into her dress pocket.

Down she dropped from branch to branch and onto Emily's shoulder.

"She likes you best, Miss Carr," said Monica.

"Well, of course," said Betty.

After a moment, Woo reached into her cheek pouch for a cherry which she gravely handed to her mistress. She kissed the woman's cheek.

"Yuk!" said Dorothy and Prue together.

"Thank you, Woo," said Miss Carr politely. Turning to the children, she added, "Woo only gives cherries to people she likes. Let's see who gets the others."

They all drew back a little. No one really wanted a cherry that had been in the monkey's mouth, but it would settle the argument about which one of them was Woo's favourite.

Allen grinned at the monkey. Prue wriggled her fingers in a little wave. Monica smirked. Dorothy and Betty each reached out a hand. Jeff sat quietly.

Woo glowered at them all. She tilted her head from side to side as she looked round the circle. She popped the other cherry out of her cheek and rubbed it on her fur to dry it.

The children held their breath as Woo's bright eyes swept over them again.

Quick as a flash, she leapt down, handed the fruit to Jeff, and scrambled to the safety of her mistress' shoulder. Then she took the third cherry from her dress pocket and ate it in dainty bites.

Miss Carr laughed at the look on Jeff's face.

"Just pretend to eat it," she said. "Like this."

She held her hand close to her mouth.

"Mmmm, it's good, Woo. Thank you," she said. She reached up to stroke the monkey's head and whispered into her ear. "And you're a clever monk, too. You know your friends."

CHAPTER FOUR

Camping in the Elephant

Woo was packing to go to camp. Years ago, Emily had given her a small tin biscuit box with a hinged lid. While Woo packed her treasures in it, she was too busy to hinder her mistress.

She had already put in a small mirror, a scrap of brightly coloured cloth with a needle stuck in it, two large pearl buttons, an empty spool, and the bristle end of a broken paint brush. In the kitchen she found two pieces of apple in her food dish. She dropped them into the box. Up on the table, she spied a package of crackers for the parrot. Jane was staying home this time. Clinging to the table leg with her two feet,

Woo pulled the package closer. The key to the apartment clattered to the floor. Emily had put it out for her sister Alice who was going to take care of things while she was away. Woo added two crackers to her tin. Then she dropped the key in, too, and closed the lid.

Emily puffed into the room.

"Your turn, Woo. The other creatures are already in their travelling boxes."

The monkey tucked the tin under her arm and took Emily's hand.

Soon she was out on the front sidewalk staring out through the bars of her cage at the piles of baggage that always went on one of the artist's camping trips.

An old truck with slatted sides chugged to a stop. Woo chattered excitedly as the driver and Emily loaded it.

"Everything but the kitchen sink, as usual," said the man in a grumpy voice.

"At least it's not raining, as usual," replied the artist cheerfully.

"It will be by the time we get there. You'll see. Never fails."

Emily handed up two easels, boxes with painting supplies, pots and pans, food, bedding, clothing, and all the paraphernalia they would need on their holiday.

At last it was time to load the animals. Woo bumped her head when she tried to stand up straight. She yelled and rubbed the sore spot.

The big case with three dogs in it was placed against one side of the truck so that the dogs could look out through the slats. Still on the sidewalk, Woo babbled and waved her hands through the bars.

Next, Suzie's little cage was wedged between two big boxes, and Dolf, the cat, was perched on the box of bedding.

"WOO! WOO! WOO!"

"Yes, yes," said Emily. "I haven't forgotten you."

She picked up the monkey's cage. Just then Alice Carr stuck her head out of the upstairs window.

"Millie, don't forget to give me the key," she called.

Emily squinted up at her.

"It's on the kitchen table," she replied.

"No, it's not. I looked there."

"It is!" said Emily.

"Is not!" said Alice.

"Oh, botheration," muttered Emily, as she handed the monkey's cage to the driver. She padded quickly around the side of the house.

Now safely in the truck, Woo grinned and chuckled. Then she settled down beside her treasure box and groomed her fur. She heard the man climb into the cab and slam the door.

After a few minutes, he muttered, "Come on, woman! What's the hold-up?"

Another few minutes passed. He beeped the horn. The two old sisters came down the sidewalk, arguing all the way.

Emily said, "It doesn't matter if the door can't be locked, Alice. There's always somebody here."

"You'll be robbed," warned Alice.

"I don't care," Emily replied crossly. "I'm going to have my holiday! Goodbye!"

Woo felt the truck sway, heard the cab door slam and the engine start. They were off to camp.

Emily Carr loved the forest. She felt lucky to live near a park and the sea, but the apartment house kept her too busy to paint. Once or twice a year she needed to get away by herself. She needed to be where she could see and hear and smell the forest. She wanted to paint the life in the huge trees.

For many years, she travelled north up the British Columbia coast to the Indian villages. When that became too difficult, she rented cabins in the woods around Victoria. Now she owned the Elephant. It was a big, clumsy caravan on wheels that could be hauled by truck to some good painting place.

This year, it sat among the huge trees in Goldstream Park, a few kilometres north of Victoria.

The artist and her animal family were delighted when the old truck rattled away at the end of the long day. In spite of the grumpy driver's prediction, it hadn't rained.

Emily set up the camp stove outside and made supper for everyone. Afterwards, with full stomachs, they all settled on the steps of the Elephant to smell the cedars and listen to the quiet. It was broken only by the gurgling of the stream, the humming of insects, and the evening song of a robin. This was a happy time for the animals because they had their mistress all to themselves.

As the light faded, a few drops of rain fell.

"Bedtime, creatures," said Emily.

She carried Woo to a big cedar tree. Just at the height of the woman's shoulders there was a hollow place. The monkey's sleeping box had been fitted inside.

"Lucky Woo!" said her mistress. "Sleeping right in the heart of a tree. You'll hear all its secrets."

Then she shut herself, the dogs, the cat, and the rat into the Elephant. Rain pattered down and lulled them all to sleep.

Woo loved camp. There were trees to climb, delicious bugs to catch, fish to watch in the stream, and lots of places to explore.

Best of all, Emily had time to spend with her pets. In the city she was always busy with house or garden or kennels or her pottery or painting. Here, even when she was absorbed in drawing, the animals could be near her. And there were long evenings and rainy days when she had only them for company.

Woo had seven very happy days.

Then a visitor arrived. She came in a car piled high with baggage.

Perched on the ridge pole of the Elephant, Woo watched while a tent was unloaded and set up. She saw the car disappear up the road, leaving a tall, slim lady behind. Woo knew her. She sometimes came to the studio and went on sketching

trips to the park or the cliffs. Woo made monkey faces and clicked her teeth.

The artist was delighted to see her friend. For the next week, the two of them worked at their drawing all day. In the evening, they talked about their work. Emily cooked special treats for the young woman.

Woo was jealous.

On the fourth day, Woo didn't bother to join the others at the painting site. She stayed in camp and teased Suzie and Dolf until they hid beyond the reach of her chain. Then she sat and pouted. Much earlier than usual, she heard the two women coming back.

She ran to meet them, but they ignored her. A bee had stung the young woman on her left arm.

For the next hour, while Woo scolded, Emily fussed over her friend. Three times she opened a tube of ointment and rubbed it gently onto the sore arm. When the monkey tried to grab the tube, Emily slapped the little black hand.

Later in the afternoon, the two artists went back into the woods to paint, taking the ointment with them. All the other animals joined the procession. Woo hid behind a stump.

When they were gone, it was very quiet

and lonely. Woo took a nap. When she awoke she was still all alone. She looked around for something to do.

What was that under the chair where the injured woman had been sitting? A tube! Woo pounced on it and jumped up on the seat.

She unscrewed the top of the tube, and a stream of thick yellow paint oozed out. Chattering happily, the monkey spread the paint on her arm. Then she squeezed the tube again and plastered the other arm. She put some on her tail, some on each leg, and some on her eyebrows.

She heard the dogs coming back. Quickly, she threw the tube and the cap into the bushes, leaned back in the chair, and grinned a welcome.

The young woman saw her first. She laughed.

"Look, Emily! A yellow monkey!" she said.

"Oh, Woo! Bad girl!" scolded Emily. "No! No! Don't lick yourself. The paint will make you sick."

Dinner was late that night. Woo had to be washed in warm water in the tin dishpan.

At home, the dogs were bathed regularly, but Woo kept herself clean the same way the cats did, by licking her hands and rubbing them over her fur. She hated getting wet all over. She whimpered and squirmed and wriggled, but she had to stay in the water until every bit of yellow paint was washed off.

Finally she was dried and wrapped in a warm sweater. She spent most of the evening in her mistress' lap.

"Don't laugh at her," said Emily to her friend. "It was my fault. She saw the fuss I made of you and she was jealous. Poor little monk."

Soon the holiday was over. It was time to pack up. Woo ran around finding treasures to put in her box.

Back home, she placed the contents one by one on the studio table in front of Emily's sister.

Alice laughed as she listed the items.

"Your sewing things. Did you have time to do needlework?

A fish head! Smelly!

A grapefruit rind. What on earth is the use of that?

A pine cone. That's nice.

A dead beetle. Oh, and a live one. Quick, Woo, catch it!

A crow's feather. Pretty.

And the door key! Oh, Woo, you monkey!"

CHAPTER FIVE

Bad Tempered Monkey

After many years of friendship between Woo and Ginger Pop, the dog died. For several days the monkey hunted for him in the garden, in the kennel, and in the apartment. Then she chose another dog friend. Not a pup, this time, but one of the full-grown males, Koko.

Now, instead of fastening Woo's leash to her own waist when they went walking, Emily often linked Woo and Koko together. If Woo wanted to stop to look at something and Koko didn't, Woo wound their chain around a board on the wooden sidewalk. Koko had to wait until the monkey was ready to move on.

One summer day, Emily led a procession down to the beach below the Dallas Road cliffs. She carried a camp stool under each arm and a canvas bag of art supplies in one hand. Next came a friend named Mary and her niece, Megan. The woman toted a picnic basket, and the child had two jugs, one with lemonade and one with water. Three griffons scampered around them.

Some distance behind, but keeping an eye on their mistress, strolled Koko and Woo, linked together by a metre-long chain. When the human heads disappeared down the cliff path, the two animals raced to catch up.

For the next hour or so, the three artists bent silently over their drawing boards. At first, the dogs and the monkey raced up and down the beach, leaping over driftwood logs and exploring behind boulders. Then they all settled down in the shade of the gorse bushes growing on the cliff face.

After a while, Megan stretched and flexed her fingers.

"I'm so hot," she said. "Could I go swimming?"

"Good idea!" said her aunt. "I'll go with you. What about you, Emily?"

"Yes, I'll wade in to cool off," she answered.

As soon as the humans moved, the animals ran over to find out what was going to happen next.

The tide had been almost full when they arrived. Now it was just beginning to go out. Woo heard Mary and Megan gasp as they stepped into the cold water. Suddenly they joined hands and ducked completely under the next wave. The dogs raced back and forth at the water's edge, barking frantically. Woo jumped up and down and squealed.

The two swimmers bobbed up and called to their friend to join them. Laughing, Emily kicked off her shoes, tucked in her skirt, and waded out up to her knees.

Eagerly, the three younger dogs swam out to her. Emily picked up a long rope of kelp and trailed it through the water in circles and figures of eight while the dogs tried to catch it.

Out in the water, humans and dogs were splashing and shouting. On shore, Koko and Woo stood barking and scolding. Emily looked back at them.

"Stop that racket, you silly creatures!" she said. "We're not drowning. We're having fun."

Koko moved closer to the water and

Woo was forced to go with him. She dipped one toe in the wave and whimpered. She shook her foot and ran back to the hot sand.

Koko waded into the water. Woo shrieked and grabbed the chain with both hands. She looked left and right but there was nothing except sand and small stones. Where could she hook the chain? The dog plowed ahead. Woo was not strong enough to hold him back. As she was dragged toward the ocean, her heels carved furrows in the sand.

When the dog was up to his belly, the waves lapped Woo's toes. She opened her mouth as wide as it would go and let out a jungle roar. Koko began to swim. With a snarl, Woo leapt on to his back and dug her hands and feet into his fur.

Emily heard his loud yelp. She laughed when she saw the monkey on his back, but she waded towards them.

"Go back, Koko," she called. "Woo doesn't like the water."

She caught hold of the dog's collar, turned him, and led him on to the beach.

Woo hopped off the dog's back and leapt up and down in rage. She scolded both the dog and the woman at the top of her voice.

Emily unhooked Woo's chain from Koko's collar.

"That's enough, now, Woo," she said. "You didn't get very wet."

Suddenly, Koko shook himself, spraying the monkey with cold water. Woo slapped him hard with both hands.

The other dogs ran to the group and all three shook themselves. Emily threw up her hands to protect her face from the shower. She dropped Woo's chain.

Woo, backing away from the dogs, found herself free. She grabbed two handfuls of sand and flung it at the dogs.

"Stop that, Woo," scolded Emily, as she stooped for the chain.

Woo ducked away and threw more sand. The dogs barked and made darting rushes at her. Megan ran out of the water and joined the chase. Woo led them on a zigzag course so that they slipped on the pebbles and skidded through the sand. At last, she escaped to the cliff and climbed into a high gorse bush. She chattered angrily at the group of enemies below.

Emily tried to coax her down. Woo made faces at her and then turned her back and groomed her wet fur. The end of the chain dangled free. Emily fastened it to a branch of the bush.

"Stay there until you're in a better temper," she said.

Woo's fur soon dried in the hot sun. She sat in the bush and pouted. She watched the swimmers come out and dry themselves. Everyone, including the dogs, had a cool drink. Then they played fetch the stick.

Emily came over to the monkey.

"Stop sulking," she said. "Come and join the fun."

Woo showed her teeth and hissed.

"Well, if that's the way you want it," said her mistress.

She went back to the others.

In a few minutes, Megan brought a striped beach ball and held it up to the monkey.

"Come and play ball with me, Woo," she coaxed.

Woo glared and stuck out her lower lip.

The women and the girl played three-corner catch while the dogs stood by to chase the ball if anyone missed. Whenever someone turned toward Woo, she pretended to be looking at a ship on the horizon.

Finally the tablecloth was laid against a driftwood log close to Woo's perch. The picnic basket was opened and the dogs were given their treats. Mary poured three cups of lemonade. Emily set out sandwiches and cake. Megan put cherries in a bowl. The three of them sat down and ate. No one called the monkey.

Woo watched them talk and laugh and eat until all the sandwiches and cake were gone. Megan reached out and took a handful of cherries. Woo dropped to the ground. Because of her chain, she couldn't quite reach the tablecloth.

"Oh, there you are, Woo," said Emily. "We missed you."

She got up, unhooked the chain, and lifted the monkey into her arms.

"Have some cherries, Woo," said Megan.

Woo took one cherry in each hand and nibbled round the stones.

Mary pulled a banana out of the basket.

"Eat up, Woo," she said. "It's almost time to go."

The monkey squatted on the edge of the cloth. With her head tilted to one side, she smiled thinly at the aunt and niece. She made kissing sounds at her mistress. Then she took the banana, peeled it, and daintily ate it.

"So, Lady Woo has forgiven us," said Emily with a laugh.

Later, Woo refused to be hooked up with Koko. Emily fastened the chain to her own waist, and the monkey rode on her shoulder at the head of the procession back to Simcoe Street. Sitting still and quiet, with her chin in the air, she looked like a dignified jungle princess being carried to her palace.

CHAPTER SIX

Poisonous Green

Emily Carr grew too old to enjoy camping out in the Elephant. She sold it and spent her painting holidays in cabins near the city.

One year she rented a cottage on the wood lot of a sheep farmer in Metchosin. For company she had two dogs, a cat called James the Second, Woo, and a large cage full of canaries. She could paint the trees in the wood or go down to the beach on the bay.

On a spit of land that jutted into the bay stood a tall dead fir tree. It had six stumpy dead branches pointing in different directions. Sometimes, a great blue heron perched on the very top of the old trunk. He sat perfectly still with his neck kinked and his beak straight out. Because his feathers were almost the same colour as the wood, he looked like another branch.

Emily decided to paint a picture of the silver-grey trunk against the dark greens of the other trees. One morning, after she had fed the animals, she carried her easel and paints across the path and set up above the beach. Woo followed her. When the artist sat down and stared quietly at the scene, Woo went in search of something more exciting.

At the cottage, Woo was not kept tied up. Now that she was old, she was less active, and she always came at her mistress' call. So, she was free to wander.

Today, she went around the back of the cabin to an ant hill she had discovered the day before. She wasn't hungry, but she swung up to a low branch and watched the ants at work. Suddenly, she heard sounds from behind her.

Snarl. Hiss! Yip! Growl.

James the Second and a raccoon were fighting fiercely.

Woo watched for a minute or two. The cat was getting the worst of it. The monkey, gibbering loudly, bounded back to Emily.

The artist was just setting out her palette.

Big daubs of white and green paint had already been squeezed on to the board. Recognizing the monkey's alarm signals, Emily dropped the tube of black and hurried after Woo.

The dogs had been staring over the fence at the sheep. They heard the uproar and came running.

Two dogs, one angry human, and a noisy monkey were too much for the raccoon. He lumbered off into the woods with the dogs after him. James the Second was left the victor in a field littered with tufts of brown, black, and grey hair. The cat's tail stopped thrashing, his fur smoothed down, and he dropped to his haunches. Licking one paw, he ran it over his right ear. When he did the same to the left one, he yowled with pain.

"Oh, poor Jem," said Emily. "That brute tore a piece out of your ear."

She picked him up.

"You'll need salve on that. The nasty brute! Poor Jem!"

After watching her fuss over the cat for a few minutes, Woo set off for the beach. On the way, she stopped beside the easel.

Usually the monkey was not allowed around the artist's supplies unless Emily was there to watch her. With a quick look over her shoulder, Woo poked at the blob of green on the palette. It was squishy. She pressed down. The paint stuck to her hand. She licked it off. Swiftly, she scooped up a handful of paint and crammed it into her mouth. Her hands were covered in green. She rubbed them on the canvas that stood ready on the easel. Then she stood back and studied the effect. She picked up some white and added that to the picture.

All at once, she felt dizzy. Her stomach hurt. She curled up under the artist's stool and moaned.

She heard a boy come whistling along the path. He was Fred, the farmer's son, bringing the daily bottle of milk to the cottage. He always took time to play with Woo.

"We've got dogs and cats on the farm," he said the first day, "and there's plenty of birds in the bush, but I've never seen a monkey before."

Woo groaned louder and soon her friend was bending over her.

"Oh," he gasped. "You've been into the paint." He knelt beside her. "Oh, Woo, did you eat it? One of our sheep died from just licking wet paint. I'll get Miss Carr."

He raced away and in a minute returned with the woman scurrying behind him.

"What next?" she exclaimed.

When she saw the monkey, Emily stood very still for a moment. Then she scooped Woo up in her arms, while issuing orders to the boy.

"Run home and ask your mother to phone the vet. Tell him Woo's eaten green paint—a lot of it. Ask him what I should do."

Just as they reached the cabin, Woo vomited.

"That's right," said her mistress. "Get rid of it."

She removed Woo's dirty dress and laid her on a towel on the table. She wiped the monkey's hands and face with the gasoline she used to thin her paints.

Poor Woo's stomach heaved and she clamped her jaws shut. Emily forced them open.

"Let it out," she said. "It's poison."

She took a rag and cleaned out the monkey's cheek pockets, the inside of her mouth, her teeth, and far down her throat.

Again the monkey retched. This time nothing came up.

"Is it all gone?" murmured Emily. She

stared down at the little body. Woo lay on her side with her legs drawn up and her long arms wrapped around her head. Her tail hung as limp as a piece of rope. From time to time she moaned softly.

Emily stirred up the fire in the stove and heated a kettle full of water. When the boy returned, she was sitting in a rocking chair on the porch with Woo lying upside down on a hot water bottle in her lap.

"What did the vet say?" called Miss Carr as soon as he appeared.

"He said to make her throw up," answered Fred.

"I did that."

The boy came up on the porch and stared at the limp animal.

"She sure looks bad," he said.

"What else did he say?" demanded Miss Carr.

"Don't let her eat any more paint."

"Pah! As if I would!" she said in disgust.

"He says she'll probably die," Fred reported. "He says green is the most poisonous."

"She will not die!" declared Emily.

The boy sat on the porch step and waited. He didn't speak again. Emily stroked her pet gently.

After a long time, Woo stirred.

"Fetch some milk, will you, Fred?" asked Miss Carr. "Let's see if she'll take it."

Woo refused the milk, an egg, soft bread, and everything else they tried to feed her.

"I know!" yelled Fred. "Wait!"

He ran in great leaps down the path.

In a very short time he was back with a jar and a package.

"It's honey and graham crackers," he gasped. "I give her that when she comes up to the house. She loves it."

Miss Carr sat Woo up in the crook of her arm.

"Get a spoon and try the honey," she said.

She held the monkey's jaws open while Fred poured in the first spoonful.

Woo swallowed and opened her mouth for more.

Fred spread some on a cracker and Woo took it in her hands and ate it in four bites. Then she licked her sticky fingers one by one.

Fred whooped with delight.

"She always does that," he yelled. "She's not going to die, is she?"

"Certainly not," said Miss Carr. "Woo has a tough stomach. She'll be fine by tomorrow."

CHAPTER SEVEN

Monkey Friends

Emily Carr was very ill. The doctor told her she must sell the apartment building and give up raising dogs. She moved with Woo, a few birds, and just two dogs to a small house. There was a back yard for Woo to run around in, a plum tree for her to climb, and children in the next house to watch. Emily had a small studio to paint in. They lived there happily for a few years.

Then Emily had another attack and went to the hospital for a long time. It was too long for the animals to be left alone. What to do with them?

The dogs and birds found homes quick-ly, but nobody wanted a fifteen-year-old monkey. Emily's sister Lizzie had died. Alice was blind. Sadly, Emily Carr decided that the best place for Woo was the monkey house at the zoo in Stanley Park in Vancouver.

One day, the man who came every day to feed and play with Woo brought her travelling case into the room with him. Many, many times, Woo had ridden in that box on a trip to camp. She climbed on top of it, grinning and chattering happily.

"Yes," said the man, "you're going for a trip. Maybe we'd better take off your dress. If the other monkeys think you're different, they may attack you."

He put a piece of woolen blanket in the bottom of the case.

"There, now, if you're cold on the ferry, you can snuggle under that."

Woo jumped in and the man closed the lid. He stroked the little black hands that grasped the bars.

"Goodbye, little monkey," he said. "I hope you'll be happy in your new home."

Soon after, another man came and loaded her on to a big truck.

Hours later, the zookeeper carried the box to the monkey house. It was a large, wire-enclosed cage divided into three compartments for three different kinds of monkeys. Each section had bars to swing on and poles to climb.

The zookeeper entered a door at the back of the middle part. He was now in a small enclosure inside the bigger section. It also had wire mesh sides. Three Javanese monkeys raced over from the big cage and clung to the wire. An older female watched from a high perch.

The zookeeper laughed.

"No, I haven't brought more food," he said. "This is a new friend for you."

He opened Woo's box and waited. Woo poked her head out and looked around. She blinked a few times.

"Woo, woo, woo," she whimpered.

"Welcome to your new home, Woo," said the man.

He kept talking quietly until the new-comer had taken a good look at the monkeys on the wire mesh, the one on the perch, and the bigger ones in the cages on either side. Then he lifted her out to the ground. She clung to his pants with one hand and peered around his leg at the chattering animals.

"I'll take off your collar," he said. "A bad monkey could grab that and choke you."

For the first time in thirteen years, Woo's neck was bare.

The man carried her to the corner and showed her a food and water dish and a bed in a wooden box.

He went away. Woo was alone in the small room. She crouched in the corner while the three monkeys jeered and howled. Once in a while, she answered with a snarl or a hiss, but she never moved closer.

Her tormenters quickly became bored and swung up to the bars to play leap-frog. Turning her back on them, Woo ate and drank.

All this time, the older monkey had watched quietly. Now, she dropped down to the ground and squatted beside the wire wall of the small room.

Woo turned, and the two animals stared at one another for a long time. Then the outside one chittered softly. Woo answered from her corner. They talked quietly until the baby monkey dropped on to his grandmother's back. The old one raced off to play with him. Woo crept into her sleeping box.

Next morning, the zookeeper took Woo by the hand and led her into the big cage.

"Let's see if they're ready to accept you," he said.

He lifted Woo up to one end of a bar.

The grandmother was sitting at the other end.

"You two ladies are about the same age," he said. "You could be friends."

He stepped back, ready to leap to Woo's rescue if necessary.

The three younger monkeys howled and made threatening gestures. The old one screamed and scolded at them. They shrank back and watched as intently as the man did.

The old one wriggled a few centimetres toward the newcomer. After a moment, Woo slid toward her. Taking turns, they came closer and closer until their shoulders touched. The grandmother reached up an arm.

Woo flinched.

Then she felt something she had not felt since she was an infant in the jungle. Her fur was being groomed by another monkey's paw. She grinned and raked her hand through the grandmother's fur.

The man smiled at her.

"That's it, then, Woo," he said. "You have a new home and a new friend."

The End

Afterword

Emily Carr was born in Victoria in 1871 and died there in 1945. For most of her life she was an artist who painted pictures of Indian villages and the rain forest. When she was too old and sick to paint, she became a writer. Her paintings and books are now among Canada's treasures.

Woo was born on the island of Java, probably in 1923. She died in Stanley Park Zoo, Vancouver, in 1938. For thirteen years, she lived with Emily Carr in Victoria.

The stories in this book are fiction, but they are based on facts written about Woo by Emily Carr and her friends. Emily wrote about her pet in letters, in her diary, and in some of her books. In *The Heart of a Peacock* she included the story, "Woo's Life."